e salty dog Shiver me

racker Blow me down

r treasure, lad Booty

r loot Yo ho ho Swab

Swashbuckler Walkin'

ail Lift up yer mugs

Scurvy skull Plunder

e drink Arr Arr Arr

Pirate Pete's
TALK LIKE A PIRATE

Pirate Pete's
TALK LIKE A PIRATE

by **Kim Kennedy** *illustrated by* **Doug Kennedy**

Abrams Books for Young Readers, New York

Pirate Pete had the most amazing ship ever to sail the high seas, but he needed a crew. Not any old crew would do, however.

"I needs me a pirate crew," Pete told his parrot. "And I know just where to find one: Rascal Island!"

"To Rascal Island we go!" cried the bird.

Pete spun the wheel toward the Sea of Mischief,
and soon his speedy ship had reached Rascal Island.

Pete dropped anchor in the bay, and then he hung
a sign across the ship's bow: BUCCANEERS WANTED.
Before long, a boat filled with rascals rowed up to
the ship. Pete rubbed his hands in glee! They were
the dirtiest, most mischievous, and sneakiest-looking
scallywags and scurvy dogs he'd ever laid his eye on.

One by one, the rascals climbed aboard the ship. "Listen up, mateys!" announced the parrot. "If ye wants to sail with Pete, then ye've gots to prove ye gots what it takes!"

Pete nodded and declared,
   "Ye needs a peg leg and an ol' eye patch,
   A fierce-lookin' hook and a beard ye can scratch!
   Ye gots to load a cannon and know how to fire it,
   But most of all, ye gots to talk like a pirate!"

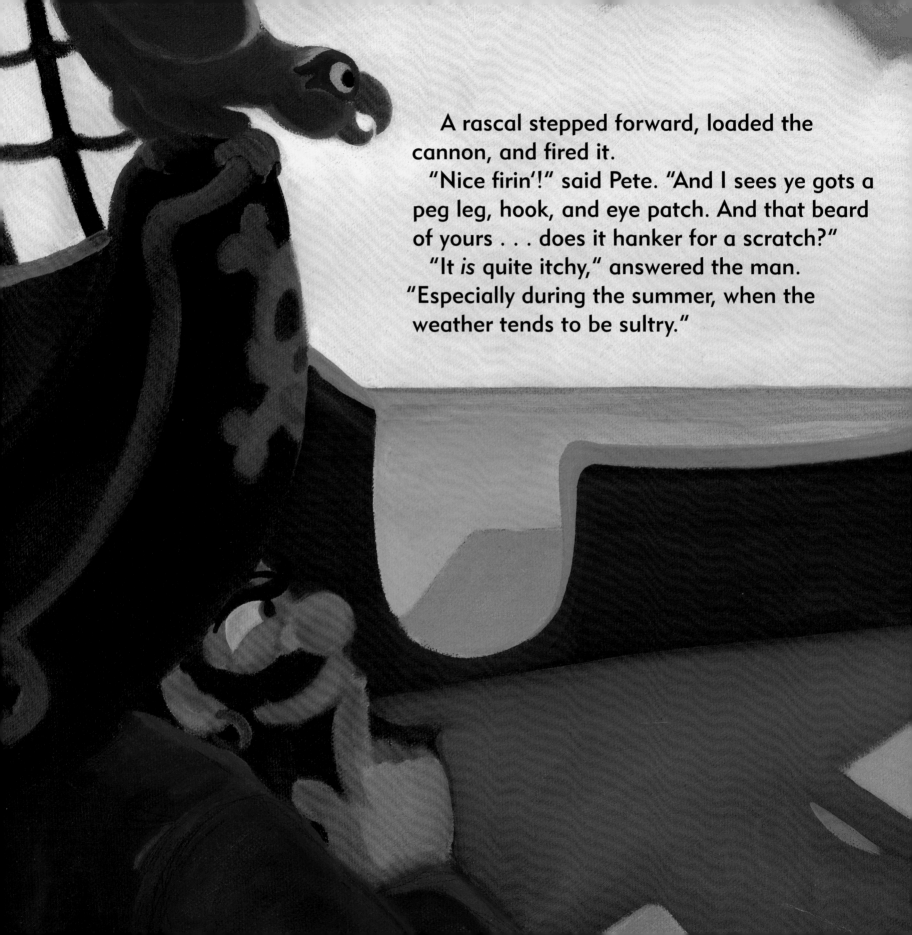

A rascal stepped forward, loaded the cannon, and fired it.

"Nice firin'!" said Pete. "And I sees ye gots a peg leg, hook, and eye patch. And that beard of yours . . . does it hanker for a scratch?"

"It *is* quite itchy," answered the man. "Especially during the summer, when the weather tends to be sultry."

"Blow me down!" bellowed Pete. "Ye don't talk like a pirate! Walk the plank!"

As the man splashed overboard, Pete hollered,
"Ye should've said,
    'When the sun's a-blazin',
    Me beard gets the itches,
    Worse than a bucket of sand down me britches!'"

"Next!" ordered the parrot.

Pete squinted at the rest of the rascals and said,
"Ye gots to be stubborn and mighty cranky,
Ye gots to be dirty and awfully stanky!
Ye gots to load a cannon and know how to fire it,
But most of all, ye gots to talk like a pirate!"

A rascal stepped forward, loaded the cannon, and fired it.

"Nice firin'!" said Pete. "And I see that yer plenty dirty and stanky. But is ye stubborn and cranky?"

"Oh, indeed!" replied the rascal. "Sometimes I'm very irritable, especially when I don't eat my breakfast."

"Shiver me timbers!" shouted Pete. "Ye don't talk like a pirate! Walk the plank!"

As the rascal went overboard, Pete cried,
"Ye should've said,
    'I's as mean as a shark
    That's stuck in a tub,
    When I've not scarfed me mornin' grub!'"

"Next!" squawked the bird.

Pete glared at the rascals and said,
"Ye gots to love treasure! Why, it's your duty
To plunder ship and shore for gleamin' booty!
Ye gots to load a cannon and know how to fire it,
But most of all, ye gots to talk like a pirate!"

A rascal stepped forward, loaded the cannon, and fired it.

"Nice firin'!" said Pete. "And judgin' by the gold and rubies yer flauntin', I reckon ye've done some plunderin' in yer day."

"That is correct," said the rascal. "I've misappropriated a number of fine jewels without permission."

"Blimey!" cried Pete. "Ye don't talk like a pirate! Walk the plank!"

As the rascal leaped overboard, Pete shouted,
"Ye should've said,
'I've pilfered loot on land and at sea,
And no man's say-so has ever stopped me!'"

"Next!" blared the parrot.

Pete shook his head. He had finally lost his patience.
He curled up his lip at the last rascal and declared,
"Ye gots to trim the sails and mind the deck,
Ye gots to be brave in case of shipwreck,
Ye gots to load a cannon and know how to fire it,
But most of all, ye gots to talk like a pirate!"

The rascal walked forward, loaded the cannon, and fired it.

"Nice firin'!" said Pete. "But is ye brave? 'Cause no lily-livered seafarer is gonna sail with me!"

"I can *assure* you that I am extremely courageous," said the rascal. "I will conduct myself with valor at all times."

"Confound it!" shouted Pete, stomping his foot. "Ye don't talk like a pirate! Walk the plank!"

As the rascal dropped overboard, Pete yelled,
"Ye should've said,
  'I've not a yellow-bellied bone
  From me head to me toes.
  I'll stand brave upon this ship wherever she goes!'"

"Can ye believe it?" Pete moaned to his parrot. "Out of all them rascals, not a one was fit for me crew."

"'Tis true!" squawked the bird. "By the powers! They's no more than a bunch o' squiffies and sprogs! None of 'em fit to go a-swashbucklin' and plunderin' for pieces of eight upon the briney blue on this here vessel!"

Pete blinked.
"Why, ye talk just like a pirate!" he cheered to
the bird. "Yer all the crew I needs. Weigh anchor!"

"Aye, aye," said the parrot, and off they sailed.

Back to the high seas went Pete and his bird.
A pirate always gets the last word!
They looked for a crew so they could hire it,
But blimey, none could talk like a pirate!

For Jackson
—Doug

For Dan
—Kim

Library of Congress Cataloging-in-Publication Data:
Kennedy, Kim.
Pirate Pete's Talk Like a Pirate / by Kim Kennedy ; illustrated by Doug Kennedy.
p. cm.
Summary: In search of a crew, Pirate Pete and his parrot look for "stanky scallywags" who possess certain conversational skills.
ISBN-13: 978-0-8109-9348-8 (hc)
ISBN-10: 0-8109-9348-1 (hc)
[1. Pirates—Fiction. 2. Parrots—Fiction.] I. Kennedy, Doug, ill. II. Title. III. Title: Talk like a pirate
PZ7.K3843Pg 2007
[E]—dc22
2006032066

Book design by Vivian Cheng

Printed and bound in China
10 9 8 7 6 5 4 3 2 1

HNA
harry n. abrams, inc.
a subsidiary of La Martinière Groupe
115 West 18th Street
New York, NY 10011
www.hnabooks.com

Har de har har Avast, timbers Polly want a Arr Arr Arr Bury, y Scallywags Lookin' f the deck Arr Arr Arr the plank Hoist the and give 'em a cheer ship and shore Into t